The BIG Blue Book of Beginner Books

by

P. D. Eastman,

R. Lopshire,

M. McClintock and F. Siebel,

M. Sadler and R. Bollen

Random House 🏠 New York

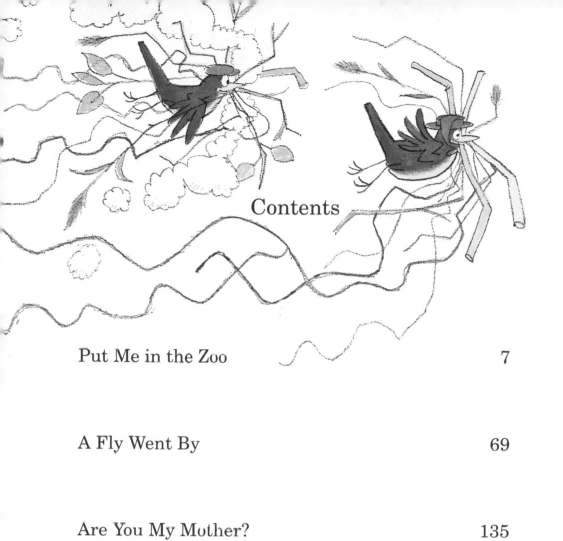

Contents

Put Me in the Zoo   7

A Fly Went By   69

Are You My Mother?   135

Go, Dog. Go!   199

The Best Nest   263

It's Not Easy Being a Bunny   327

Put Me in the Zoo

by Robert Lopshire

To Ted, Helen and Phyllis

I will go into the zoo.

I want to see it.

Yes, I do.

I would like to
live this way.
This is where
I want to stay.

Will you keep me
in the zoo?
I want to stay
in here with you.

We do not want you
in the zoo.
Out you go!
Out! Out with you.

Why did they
put me out this way?
I should be in.
I want to stay.

Why should they
put you in the zoo?
What good are you?
What can you do?

What good am I?

What can I do?

Now here is one thing
I can do.

20

Look! Now all his spots
are blue!

And now his spots are orange!

Say!

He looks very good

that way.

Now look at this!

What do you see?

Green spots! As green
as green can be!

Violet spots!

Say! You are good!

Do more! Do more!

We wish you would.

I can do more.
Look! This is new.
Blue, orange, green,
and violet, too.

Oh! They would put me
in the zoo,
if they could see
what I can do.

I can put my spots
up on this ball.

And I can put them
on a wall.

I can put them
on a cat
And I can put them
on a hat.

I can put them
on the zoo!

And I can put
my spots on you!

Look at this, now!
One! Two! Three!

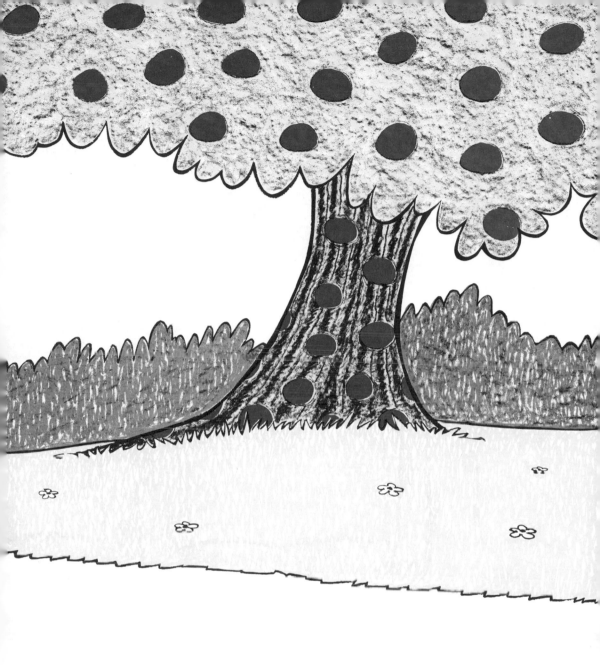

I can put them
on a tree.

And now

when I say "One, two, three"

All my spots
are back on me!

Look, now!
Here is one thing more.
I take my spots.
I make them four.

Oh! They would put me
in the zoo,
if they could see
what I can do.

I take my spots,
I take them all,

And I can make them
very small.

And now, you see,
I take them all
and I can make them
very tall.

And when I want
to have more fun,
I take my spots
and make them one.

Yes, they should put me
in the zoo.
The things my spots
and I can do!

See! I can put them
in a box.

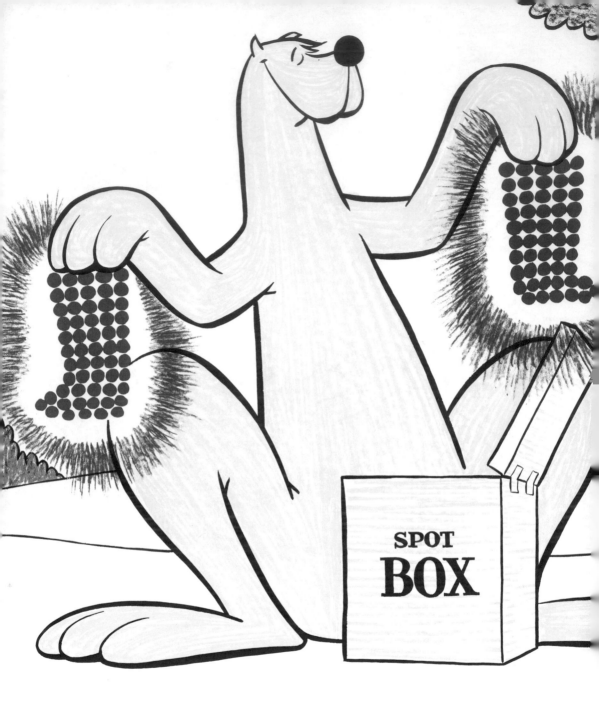

I take them out.

They look like socks.

52

And I can put them
way up high.
Up, up they go!
I make them fly.

I put them
high up in the air.
My spots fly here.
My spots fly there.

I call them back, now,
One! Two! Three!

Now all my spots
are back with me.
Tell me. Tell me, now,
you two.
Do you like
the things I do?

Tell me. Tell me, now,
you two.
Will they put me
in the zoo?

We like all
the things you do.
We like your spots,
we like you, too.

But
you should not
be in the zoo.
No. You should NOT
be in the zoo.

With all the things
that you can do,
the circus
is the place
for you!

Yes!
This is where
I want to be.
The circus is
the place for me!

A FLY WENT BY

by Mike McClintock
Illustrated by Fritz Siebel

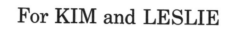

For KIM and LESLIE

I sat by the lake.

I looked at the sky,

And as I looked,

A fly went by.

A fly went by.

He said, "Oh, dear!"

I saw him shake.

He shook with fear.

And when I saw that fly go past,

I asked him why he went so fast.

I asked him why he shook with fear.

I asked him why he said, "Oh, dear!"

He said, "I MUST GET OUT OF HERE!"

The fly said, "LOOK!
And you will see!
That frog!
That frog is after me!"

The fly went past!
The frog came . . . FAST!

I asked the frog,

I asked him, "Why——?

WHY DO YOU WANT TO GET THAT FLY?"

The frog said, "Me?
I want no fly.
But I must hop,
And this is why . . ."

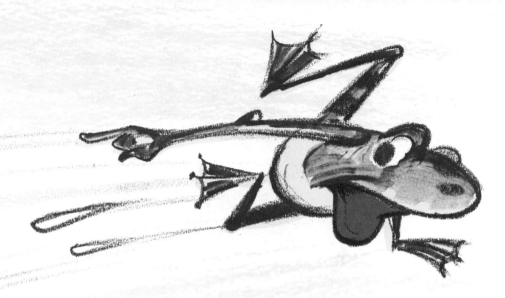

"That cat!" he said. "Just look and see!
That cat," he said, "is after me!"

Then he was gone
With one big hop.
The cat ran up,
And I said, "STOP!

Now, stop! Stop! Stop!" I told the cat.
"Do not pick on the frog like that!"

The cat said,

"Look, I want no frog.

I have to get away from . . .

SO . . .

The fly ran away
In fear of the frog,
Who ran from the cat,
Who ran from the dog.

One ran from the other.

The other ran, too,

From one who came after.

Now what could I do?

Away past the lake
Went the fly and the frog.
Away past the lake
Ran the cat and the dog.

They went past a shcd,
And they went up a hill.
I ran!   And I said,
"I will stop them, I will!

The fly does not know that the frog is not mad.
The frog does not know that the cat is not bad.
The cat runs in fear of the dog, I can tell.
If I can stop HIM, then all will be well!"

I ran a lot.

I ran so fast,

I came up to the dog at last.

"Now, stop!" I said.

"You are the one

Who did all this!

Why do you run?

Why do you want to bite that cat?

Oh, you are bad to be like that!"

The dog said, "No! That is not so!

I want no cat.

The cat can go.

I do not want to bite the cat!

I run to get away from THAT!"

"That pig!" he said.

"Look back and see!

SHE likes to bite,

And she wants ME!"

SO . . .

The fly ran away
In fear of the frog,
Who ran from the cat,
Who ran from the dog.

The dog ran away

In fear of the pig.

My, she was mad!

And WAS she big!!

I said to the pig,

"So YOU are the one

In back of all this!

Now, why do you run?

Now, why should a pig bite a dog?" I said.

"And why are you mad?

Are you out of your head?"

The pig said, "I am NOT out of my head!
See what is after me! Look!" she said.

"That cow will hit me," said the pig.

"Those things up on her head are big!"

So the pig ran past.

She ran past . . . FAST!

Then the cow ran up,

And a little cow, too.

I said, "Now what got into you?

Do not pick on the pig, you two!"

The cow said, "Pig? The pig can go!

That is not why we run—oh, no!

But some one bad has made us run!

He wants to kill my Little One!"

100

I asked the cow,
"Who wants to kill
Your Little One?
Why, no one will!"

The cow said, "Look!
Up on the hill!
The fox is there!
He comes to kill!"

The cow and little cow ran past.
All full of fear they ran past

...FAST!

SO . . .

The fly ran away
In fear of the frog,
Who ran from the cat,
Who ran from the dog.
The dog ran away
From the pig—and now
The pig ran away
In fear of the cow!

They came to the woods,

And there was a tent.

But they did not stop!

In and out they all went!

And last came the fox,

So HE was the one

Who made them all fear,

And made them all run!

Yes, he was the one who was bad, I could tell.

If I could stop HIM, then all would be well!

I told the fox,

"Oh, shame on you!

Oh, shame, shame, shame

For what you do!

You want to kill the little cow!

You stop, or I will whip you—NOW!"

The fox said, "Now what did I do?

Why do you say, 'Oh, shame on you'?

I tell you I would never kill

That little cow!

I never will!"

The fox said, "This is why I ran——
Back in the woods I saw a man!
I saw a man!
He had a gun!

He wants to get me!
Let me run!"

SO . . .

The fly ran away
In fear of the frog,
Who ran from the cat,
Who ran from the dog.
The dog and the pig
And the cows—they all ran!
And then came the fox,
Who ran from the man!

They came to a house
And went down the hall.
And when they went out,
There was a big wall.
But that did not stop them.
Oh, no—not at all!

111

They ran and they ran.
They came to a town.
They went up one way,
And then they went down.

They went up one way,
And then down another.
They ran and they ran,
One after the other.

They came to a bank,
But they did not stop.
They went in the bank
With a jump and a hop!

With a jump and a hop
They ran in—and then
They went out the back way,
And ran on again!

I ran as fast
As I could run.
I told the man,
"YOU are the one
In back of this!
You are the one
Who wants the fox!
Put down your gun!"

"Fox? Fox?" the man said. "No!

I saw no fox,

But I must go!

For you should see,

Yes, you should see

The thing that now is after ME!"

"I did not see it," said the man.

"I took my gun and then I ran.

For I could hear it bump and thump

It was so bad it made me jump!

It was so bad it made me fear!

It was so big! It was so near!

It must be ten feet tall!" he said,

"And big and fat and bad and red!

Why, it can bite and kick and kill!

And it will do it! Yes, it will!

I hear it now! Come on, I say!

For I must run and get away!"

"BUMP!"
"THUMP!"

The man ran past
Fast . . . Fast . . . FAST!

What did I hear? A bump and thump!
It was so bad it made me jump!
I was about to run away,
But then I saw the thing—and, SAY!

It <u>was</u> not tall!
It <u>was</u> not mad!
It <u>was</u> not big!
It <u>was</u> not bad!

Was THIS the thing
That made them run,
And made them fear?
Was THIS the one?

It was a little sheep! So tame!

It came to me, and it was lame!

I saw what made the bump and thump.

I saw the thing that made me jump.

The sheep said, "Look at this tin can!

I can not get it off! I ran!

I ran for help! I saw a man.

I went to him, but then HE ran!

Why did he run away from me?

I just want help, as you can see."

I said, "I will get help for you!
And I can help the others, too!
For now I know just what to do!"

"Oh, man!" I called. "Come back! Come here!
This is a sheep, so have no fear!
The sheep wants help, for it is lame.
Come back! Come here!"

And then he came!

And then the man
Took off the can.

But still the others ran and ran.

They did not know about the can.

I had to call so they would hear.

I had to tell them not to fear.

I had to tell them all was well.

And so I gave a great big yell . . .

I said to them all, "You must not run away!
No one is after you! No one, I say!
You all ran away—and now I know why.
I sat by the lake, and there came a fly.

The fly ran away
In fear of the frog,
Who ran from the cat,
Who ran from the dog.
The dog ran away
In fear of the pig,
Who ran from the cow.
She was so big!
The cow ran away
From the fox, who ran
As fast as he could
In fear of the man.
That man heard a thump,
And away he ran!
It was just a sheep,
With an old tin can!"

I looked at them all,
And then I could tell
They all had no fear,
And now all was well.

They all went away.

They all waved good–by.

SO . . .

I sat by the lake
And looked at the sky.

Are You My Mother?

Written and Illustrated by
P. D. EASTMAN

To My Mother

A mother bird sat on her egg.

The egg jumped.

"Oh oh!" said the
mother bird. "My baby
will be here! He will
want to eat."

"I must get something
for my baby bird to
eat!" she said. "I will be
back!"

So away she went.

The egg jumped. It
jumped, and jumped, and
jumped!

Out came the baby
bird!

"Where is my mother?"
he said.

He looked for her.

He looked up. He did
not see her.

He looked down. He did
not see her.

"I will go and look for her," he said.

So away he went.

Down, out of the tree
he went.

Down, down, down! It
was a long way down.

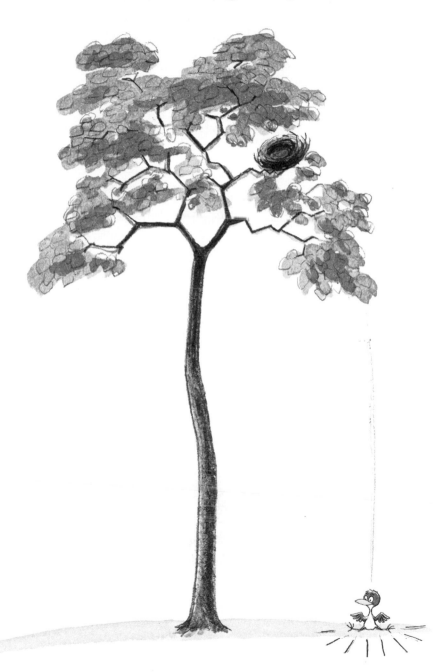

The baby bird could
not fly.

He could not fly, but
he could walk. "Now I
will go and find my
mother," he said.

He did not know what
his mother looked like. He
went right by her. He did
not see her.

He came to a kitten.
"Are you my mother?"
he said to the kitten.

The kitten just looked
and looked. It did not
say a thing.

The kitten was not his
mother, so he went on.

Then he came to a
hen.

"Are you my mother?"
he said to the hen.

"No," said the hen.

The kitten was not
his mother.

The hen was not
his mother.

So the baby bird went on.

"I have to find my
mother!" he said. "But
where? Where is she?
Where could she be?"

Then he came to a
dog.

"Are you my mother?"
he said to the dog.

"I am not your mother.

I am a dog," said the dog.

The kitten was not
his mother.

The hen was not
his mother.

The dog was not
his mother.

So the baby bird went
on. Now he came to a
cow.

"Are you my mother?"
he said to the cow.

"How could I be your
mother?" said the cow. "I
am a cow."

The kitten and the hen
were not his mother.

The dog and the cow
were not his mother.

Did he have a mother?

"I did have a mother," said the baby bird. "I know I did. I have to find her. I will. I WILL!"

Now the baby bird did
not walk. He ran!

Then he saw a car.
Could that old thing be
his mother? No, it could not.

The baby bird did not
stop. He ran on and on.

Now he looked way,
way down. He saw a
boat. "There she is!" said
the baby bird.

He called to the boat,
but the boat did not
stop.

The boat went on.

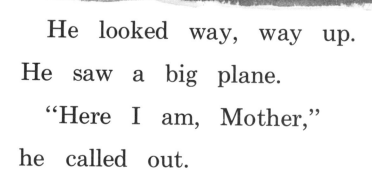

He looked way, way up.

He saw a big plane.

"Here I am, Mother,"

he called out.

But the plane did not
stop. The plane went on.

Just then, the baby bird
saw a big thing. This
must be his mother!

"There she is!" he said.
"There is my mother!"

He ran right up to it.
"Mother, Mother! Here
I am, Mother!" he said
to the big thing.

181

But the big thing just said, "Snort."

"Oh, you are not my mother," said the baby bird. "You are a Snort. I have to get out of here!"

183

But the baby bird could
not get away. The Snort
went up.

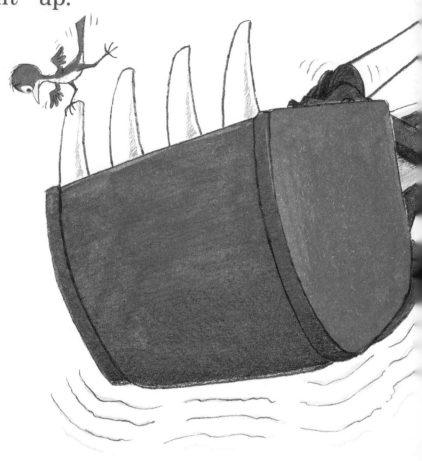

It went way, way up.

And up, up, up went

the baby bird.

But now, where was
the Snort going?

"Oh, oh, oh! What is
this Snort going to do to
me? Get me out of here!"

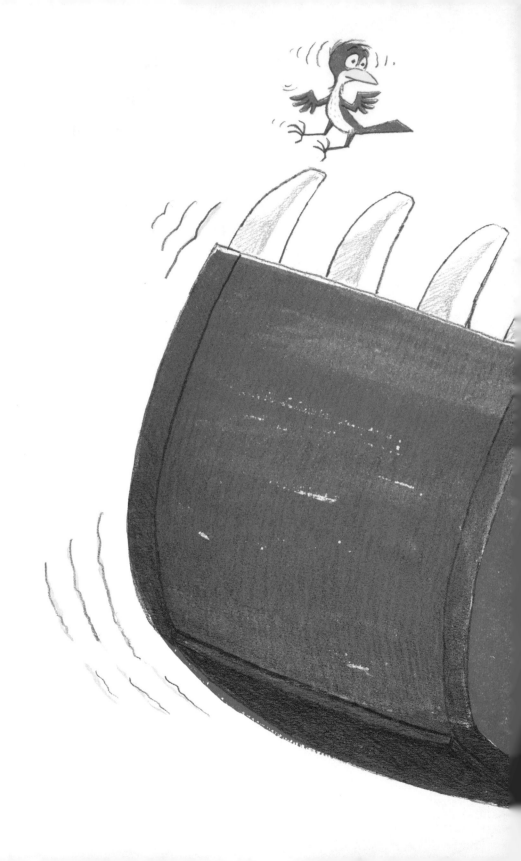

Just then, the Snort
came to a stop.

190

"Where am I?" said the
baby bird. "I want to go
home! I want my
mother!"

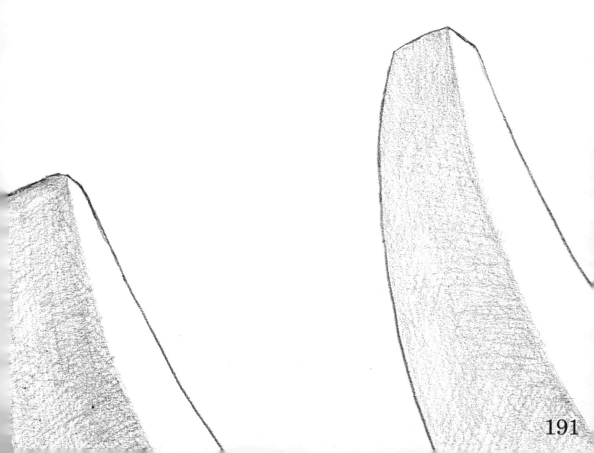

Then something
happened.

The Snort put that
baby bird right back in
the tree. The
baby bird was home!

Just then the mother bird came back to the tree. "Do you know who I am?" she said to her baby.

"Yes, I know who you are," said the baby bird.

"You are not a kitten.

"You are not a hen.

"You are not a dog.

"You are not a cow.

"You are not a boat, or a plane, or a Snort!"

"You are a bird, and you are my mother."

197

Go, Dog. Go!

by P.D. Eastman

To Cluny

Dog.

Big dog.

Little dog.

Big dogs and little dogs.

Black and white dogs.

"Hello!"

"Hello!"

"Do you like my hat?"

"I

do

not."

"Good-by!"

"Good-by!"

One little dog going in.

Three big dogs going out.

A red dog
on a blue tree.

A blue dog
on a red tree.

A green dog
on a yellow tree.

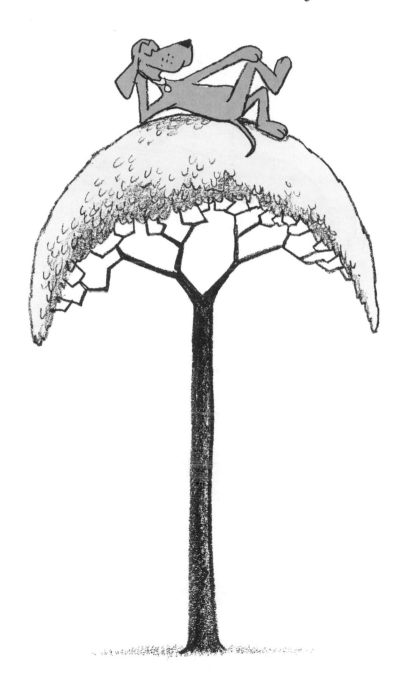

Some big dogs
and some little dogs
going around
in cars.

A dog

out of a car.

Two big dogs
going up.

One little dog
going down.

The green dog
is up.

The yellow dog
is down.

The blue dog
is in.

The red dog
is out.

One dog up
on a house.

Three dogs down
in the water.

A green dog
over a tree.

A yellow dog
under a tree.

Two dogs

in a house

on a boat

in the water.

A dog over the water.

A dog under the water.

"Hello again."

"Hello."

"Do you like
my hat?"

"I do not
like it."

"Good-by again."

"Good-by."

The dogs
are all going
around,
and around,
and around.

"Go around
again!"

The sun is up.

The sun is yellow.

The yellow sun

is over the house.

"It is hot
out here in
the sun."

"It is not hot
here under the house."

Now it is night.

Three dogs
at a party
on a boat
at night.

Dogs at work.

Work, dogs,
work!

232

Dogs at play.

"Play, dogs, play!"

"Hello again."

"Hello."

"Do you
like my hat?"

"I do not
like that hat."

"Good-by again."

"Good-by!"

Dogs in cars again.

Going away.

Going away fast.

Look at those dogs go.
Go, dogs. Go!

"Stop, dogs. Stop!
The light is red now."

"Go, dogs. Go!

The light is green now."

Two dogs at play.

At play up on top.

"Go down, dogs.

Do not play up there.

Go down."

Now it is night.

Night is not

a time for play.

It is time for sleep.

The dogs go to sleep.

They will sleep all night.

Now it is day.

The sun is up.

Now is the time

for all dogs to get up.

"Get up!"
It is day.
Time to get going.
Go, dogs. Go!

There they go.

Look at those dogs go!

Why are they going fast
in those cars?
What are they going to do?
Where are those dogs going?

Look where they are going.
They are all going to that
big tree over there.

Now the cars stop.
Now all the dogs get out.
And now look where
those dogs are going!

To the tree! To the tree!

Up the tree! Up the tree!

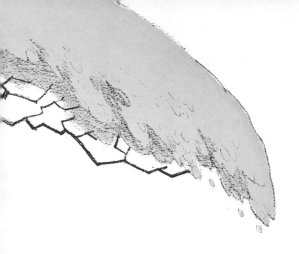

Up they go
to the top of the tree.
Why?
Will they work there?
Will they play there?
What is up there
on top of that tree?

A dog party!

A big dog party!

Big dogs, little dogs,

red dogs, blue dogs,

yellow dogs, green dogs,

black dogs, and white dogs

are all at a dog party!

What a dog party!

"Hello again.
And now
do you
like
my hat?"

"I do.
What a hat!
I like it!
I like
that party hat!"

"Good-by!"

"Good-by."

262

The Best Nest

Written and Illustrated by

P. D. EASTMAN

To H. P. G.

Mr. Bird was happy.

He was so happy he had to sing.

This was Mr. Bird's song:

"I love my house.

I love my nest.

In all the world

My nest is best!"

Then Mrs. Bird came
out of the house.
"It's NOT the best
nest!" she said.

"I'm tired of this old place,"
said Mrs. Bird. "I hate it.
Let's look for a new place
right now!"

So they left the old place
to look for a new one.

"This place looks nice,"
said Mr. Bird.
"Let's move in here."

But somebody else
had already moved in.

So they looked at another house.
"This one looks nice," said Mr. Bird.
"And there's nobody in it."

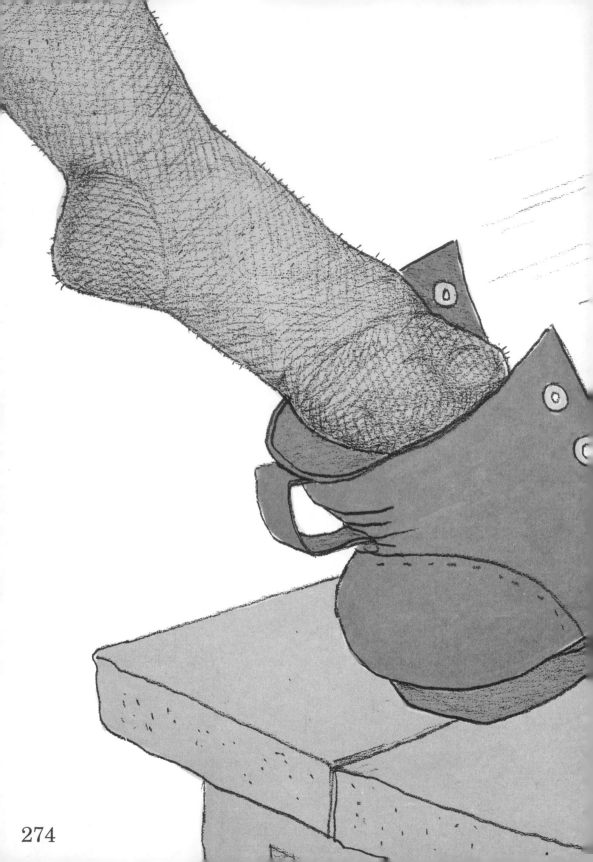

"You're wrong," said Mrs. Bird.
"This house belongs to a foot!"

So they went on looking.

"I like this one," said Mr. Bird.

"It has a pretty red flag

on the roof."

"I've always wanted a house
with a flag," said Mrs. Bird.
"Maybe this place will be
all right."

But it was not all right!
"I guess I made a mistake,"
said Mr. Bird.

"You make too many mistakes,"
said Mrs. Bird.
"I'm going to pick the next house.

"And here it is—right here!"

They flew in.
They looked around.
"Isn't it too big?"
asked Mr. Bird.

"I like this big place,"
said Mrs. Bird. "This is the place
to build our new nest."

They went right to work.
They needed many things
to build their nest.
First they got some hay.

They got some soda straws

and broom straws.

They got some sweater string.

They got some stocking string . . .

. . . and mattress stuffing.

They got some horse hair.

They got some man hair.

Soon they had all the hay,
all the straw, all the string,
all the stuffing, all the
horse hair, and all the man hair
they could carry.
They took it all back
to build their nest.

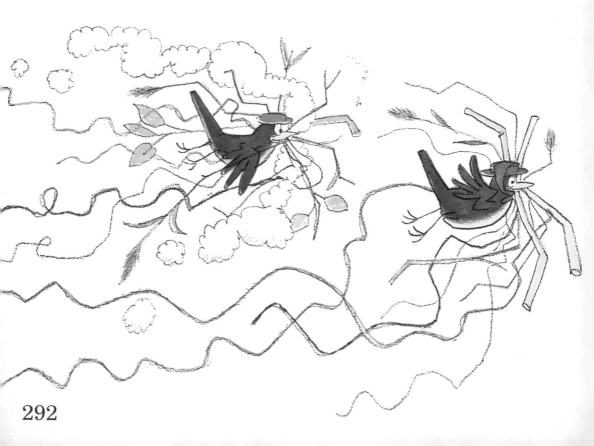

Mr. and Mrs. Bird worked very hard.
It took them the rest of the
morning to finish their nest.

"This nest is really the best!"
said Mrs. Bird.

"I want to stay here forever."

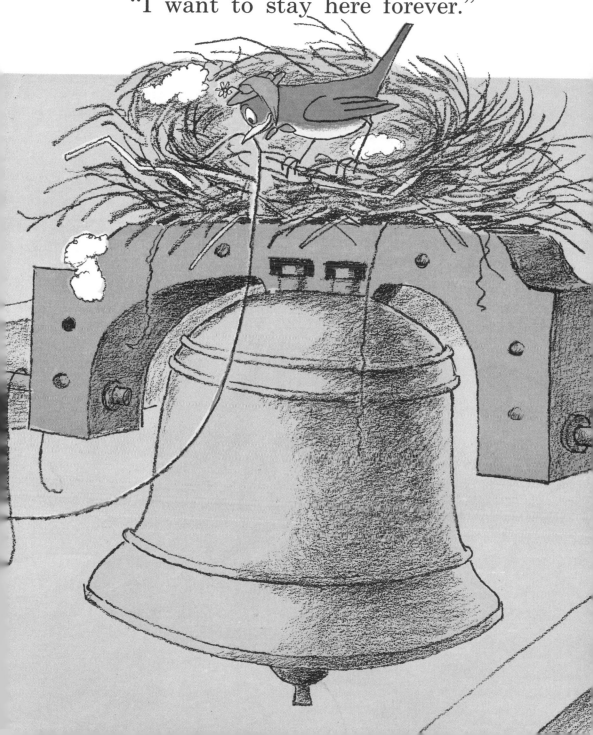

Mr. Bird was very happy too.

He flew to the top of his house.

He sang his song again:

"I love our house.

I love our nest.

In all the world

Our nest is best!"

He was so busy singing, he didn't
even see Mr. Parker coming.

Every day at twelve o'clock,

Mr. Parker came to the church.

Mr. Parker came to pull a rope.

The rope went up

to the Birds' new nest.

The rope rang the big bell
right under Mrs. Bird's nest.

BONG

Mrs. Bird got out of there
as fast as she could fly.

When Mr. Bird came in,
all he could see was a mess
of hay and string and stuffing
and horse hair and man hair
and straws. Where was Mrs. Bird?

"I will look for her until I find her,"
said Mr. Bird. He looked high.
He looked low.
He looked everywhere for Mrs. Bird.

He looked down into a chimney.
But Mrs. Bird wasn't there.

He looked down into a water barrel.
But Mrs. Bird wasn't there.

Then he saw a big fat cat.
There was a big fat smile
on the fat cat's face.
There were some pretty brown feathers
near the fat cat's mouth.

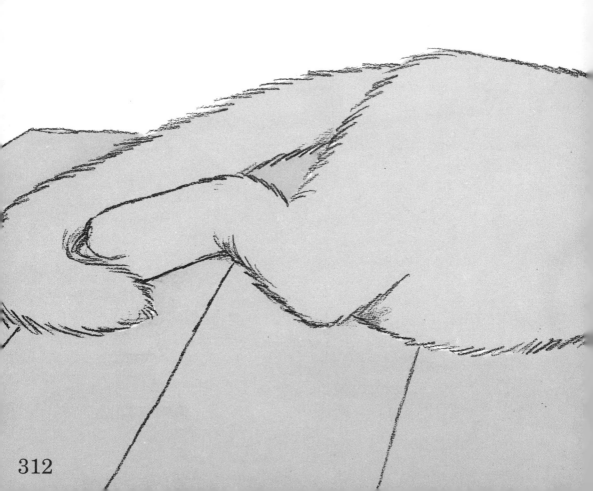

Mr. Bird began to cry.

"Oh, dear!" he cried.

"This big fat cat has eaten Mrs. Bird!"

Mr. Bird flew off.

"I'll never see
Mrs. Bird again," he cried.

It was getting dark.

It began to rain.

It rained harder and harder.

Mr. Bird could not see
where he was going.

Crash!

Mr. Bird bumped into something!

It was his old house—
that old, old house that Mrs. Bird hated.

"I'll go inside," said Mr Bird.

"I'll rest here until the rain stops."

Mr. Bird went in.

And there was Mrs. Bird!

Sitting there,

singing!

"I love my house.

I love my nest.

In all the world

This nest is best."

"*You! Here!*" gasped Mr. Bird.

"I thought you hated this old nest!"

Mrs. Bird smiled.

"I used to hate it," she said.

"But a mother bird

can change her mind.

You see . .

. . . there's no nest
like an old nest—
for a brand-new bird!"

And when the egg popped open,
the new bird thought so too!

It's Not Easy Being a Bunny

by Marilyn Sadler

illustrated by
Roger Bollen

P. J. Funnybunny was very sad.

He did not like being a bunny.

His mother made him eat
cooked carrots every day.

He had far too many
brothers and sisters.

And his ears
were very big.

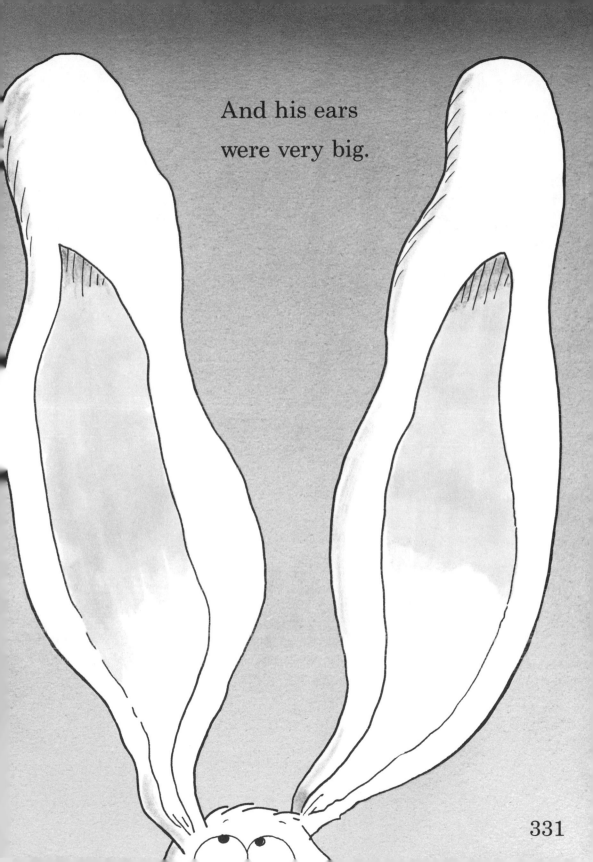

One day P. J. decided
to leave home.

"I don't want to be
a bunny anymore,"
said P. J.

"I want to be a...

...BEAR!"

And P. J. went to live
with the bears.

But when the bears
went to sleep
for the winter,
P. J. could not sleep
at all.
Living with the bears
was not very exciting.

So P. J. said,

"I don't want to be a bear.

I want to be a...

...BIRD!"

And P. J. went to live
with the birds.

P. J. liked being a bird—
until he tried to fly.

So P. J. said,
"I don't want to be a bear
OR a bird.

I want to be a...

And P. J. went to live
with the beavers.

The beavers liked to work
very hard.
P. J. did not like to work
at all.

So P. J. said,

"I don't want to be a bear

or a bird

OR a beaver.

I want to be a…

...PIG!"

And P. J. went to live
with the pigs.

But the only thing
the pigs liked to do
was sit in the mud.

So P. J. said,

"I don't want to be a bear

or a bird

or a beaver

OR a pig.

I want to be a...

...MOOSE!"

And P. J. went to live
with the moose.

But P. J. could not make
good moose calls.

So P. J. said,

"I don't want to be a bear

or a bird

or a beaver

or a pig

OR a moose.

I want to be a...

...POSSUM!"

And P. J. went to live
with the possums.

The possums liked to hang
upside down.
But hanging upside down
gave P. J. a headache.

So P. J. said,

"I don't want to be a bear

or a bird

or a beaver

or a pig

or a moose

OR a possum.

I want to be a...

...SKUNK!"

And P. J. went to live
with the skunks.

It did not take P. J. very long
to find out that he did not like
living with the skunks.

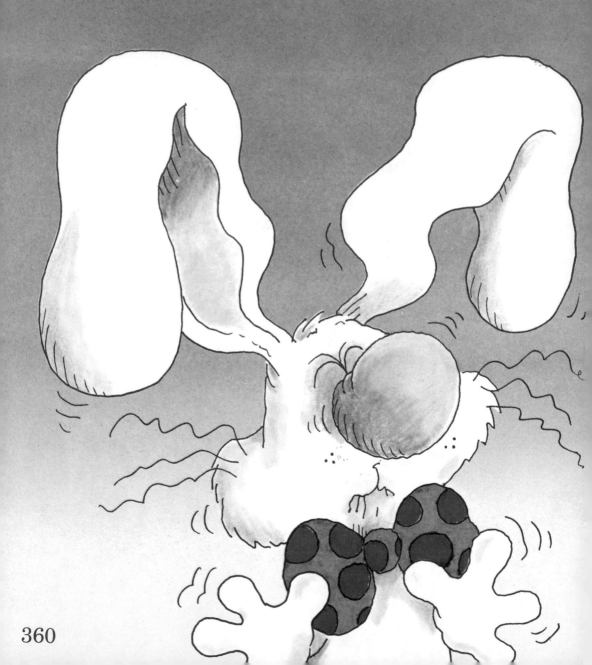

So P. J. said,
"I don't want to be a bear
or a bird
or a beaver
or a pig
or a moose
or a possum
OR, most of all, a skunk.

What I REALLY want to be is a...

So P. J. hurried home.
The Funnybunnies were very happy
to see him.
P. J. was very happy
to see them.

That night P. J. ate

all of his cooked carrots...

...and played with every one

of his brothers and sisters.

He was so happy
to be a bunny again
that he did not care
that his ears were very big.
"At least everyone can see
that I am a bunny," P. J. said,
"and not a...

...bear

or a bird

or a beaver

or a pig

or a moose

or a possum

or a skunk."